Library of Congress Control Number: 2021936735

Published by:

Chin Music Press
1501 Pike Place #329
Seattle, WA 98101-1542
www.chinmusicpress.com

First (1) edition
Design by Carla Girard
Printed in Canada

ISBN: 978-1-63405-979-4

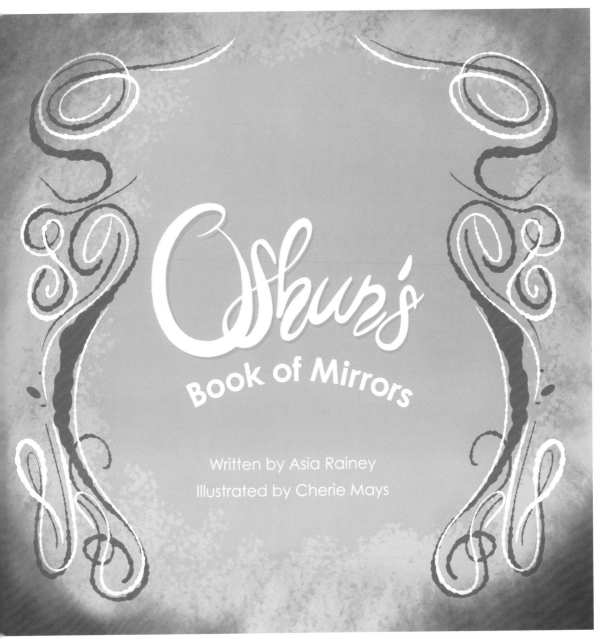

Oshun's

Book of Mirrors

Written by Asia Rainey

Illustrated by Cherie Mays

Dedicated to
Gavyn & Gabryel Rainey

In Celebration of Paris

There once was a little girl named Oshun who lived in a dark forest. Her friends were the animals who roamed all around.

They were once carefree and happy, but the animals now only knew of ugly things and of hurtful words—they did not know any better. Darkness was all they could see.

The forest had been dark for a long, long time, and they could no longer see the good in the world.

She did not remember the bright sun, or the blooming flowers, or the sounds of laughter. The darkness had come and hidden all of the wondrous things away.

The animals were all that Oshun had to keep her company in the dark forest.

Every day, Oshun would wander from home into the forest. She wondered about everything. She wanted to know why the forest was what it was. Every why and because, she wondered.

And most of all, Oshun wondered, "Who am I?"

On one particular day, Oshun decided to ask the animals to tell her who she was. She thought, "Maybe if I learn who I am, I will know how to bring the light back to the forest."

She walked down a path through the trees, and she came to the Baboon. She said to him, "Baboon, can you tell me who I am?"

The Baboon was so used to being laughed at for his squinch-y face and big, furry body. He knew no better than to tell Oshun what he knew.

"You are ugly, is what you are," the Baboon said. "This is all I see." Oshun thought for a moment, and said, "I do not feel ugly, but you must see better than me." She thanked the Baboon and went on down the path.

Soon, she came to the Elephant grazing quietly among the trees. Oshun said to her, "Elephant, can you tell me who I am?"

All of the other animals had told the Elephant that she was not wise, and the Elephant knew no better than to tell Oshun what she knew.

The Elephant said to Oshun, "You are not smart, is what you are, for this is all I see."

Oshun thought for a long moment, and said, "I do not feel that I am not smart, but you must see better than me." She thanked the Elephant and went on down the path.

Then, she came to a teeny, tiny Ant. Oshun crouched down to the Ant and said, "Ant, can you tell me who I am?" The Ant had been told all its life that it was the smallest thing, and couldn't possibly be strong, so it knew no better than to tell Oshun what it knew.

The Ant said, "You are weak, is what you are, for this is all I see." Oshun thought for just a moment, and said, "I do not feel weak, but you must see better than me."

Now on this day, Oshun had walked so far down the path through the dark forest that she came to a River she had never seen before.

Yet as soon as she saw its waters, she realized this must be the River that all of the animals had said was lost long ago.

It had been lost along with the flowers, and the sounds of laughter. She remembered the stories of the River, of its magic. It was able to answer any question.

But Oshun had only one question to ask.

She walked down to the waters and said, "Oh River, can you tell me who I am?"

The waves in the River rippled, and then rose high into the air. River said, "Greetings, Oshun my daughter, I can answer your question with my water."

A square of water broke free from the River, and it hung in mid-air with the shimmer of a mirror.

As Oshun stared into the water mirror, she heard a tinkling of chimes begin to ring, and the River began to sing in an ancient tongue, "Ide were were nita Oshun, ide were were nita Iya…"

Then the water mirror floated over the waves until it reached Oshun, and it landed into her hands. She thought the water would run through her fingers, but it formed into a little book in her palms.

Oshun opened the book, hoping to read a great answer to her question, but all of the pages were blank.

Surprised, she asked the River, "But what is this? How can this empty book tell me who I am?"

The River said, "Ah, Oshun, this is your Book of Mirrors, to be filled with who you want to be. Oshun, fill the Book of Mirrors with the little girl you want to see."

Oshun sat down next to the River and began to speak words that formed onto each page.

She said:

"Beautiful… smart… strong…

…kind… funny… creative… and unique!"

Now when Oshun looked at the book, she began to see more than the words she spoke. She saw herself in the Book of Mirrors.

When she looked up from the book, the forest had begun to brighten with the rays of the sun, the flowers had started to bloom again, and she could hear the sound of laughter on the breeze.

Oshun giggled with joy as the forest changed around her. She rose and turned to the River and said, "Thank you, River, for your wonderful gift!" But River had already settled back into her soft waves, moving on upstream.

Oshun ran back into the forest with her Book of Mirrors, marveling at the colors sprouting from the earth and the touch of sweet breeze brushing her cheeks.

She ran so fast that she almost stumbled upon the Ant, who was struggling with a morsel of food. She watched as the Ant pulled the crumb of food, twice as big as its own body, onto its back.

Oshun opened her Book to the Ant and said, "Ah, Ant, but don't you see? You are quite strong, just like me." Ant stopped to look into the Book of Mirrors, and saw that it could carry much more than most. It said, "Yes, Oshun, I see!"

Oshun laughed and continued her run through the forest, twirling and skipping as the trees opened up to the sun. There, she saw the Elephant, standing quietly in the grass.

Oshun went right up to the Elephant, and held the Book up high. She said, "Elephants never forget the wisdom of the ancestors, and I can see it in your eyes. You are smart, my friend, don't you see? You are wise, just like me."

The Elephant looked into the Book and saw her own eyes. She said to Oshun, "Yes, I see!"

Now, Oshun was so close to home, and she was amazed at the wonders opening along the path. From stones to flowers to blades of grass, everything had its own beauty to behold.

Then, Oshun heard a soft sound of crying, and she realized it was the Baboon sitting under a tree.

She said to the Baboon, "Ah, Baboon, why do you cry? Do you not see the darkness melting from the sky?"

The Baboon looked up at Oshun and said, "Oshun, until today, my squinch-y face and big, furry body was as ugly as the dark forest. Ugly was all I could see. Now, everything around me is so beautiful. The only ugly thing is me."

Oshun took a long look at the Baboon, and then at her Book of Mirrors. She turned the Book to the Baboon so he could see himself in its pages.

She spoke to him softly, "Ah Baboon, but don't you see? You are different, and magnificent, and beautiful in your very own way. Just like me."

The Baboon saw himself in the Book, and looked up at Oshun. He smiled a wide grin, and watched as Oshun ran off towards home with her Book of Mirrors in hand.

As she ran through the forest, Oshun spoke beautiful things into the mirror. With every word she spoke, beautiful things continued to grow, as if the forest finally remembered how full of light it could be.

So from that day on, Oshun spoke beauty into every place and every thing, and beautiful is all she could see.

Asia Rainey is a multidisciplinary artist and writer with a resume spanning spoken word poetry, music, theatre, visual arts, and film. As a native New Orleanian, her work reflects the vivid vernacular, southern rhythm, and spirited culture of her birthplace. Known for writing with intense imagery and lyrical storytelling, Rainey has been welcomed as a dynamic performer at numerous events, festivals, and educational institutions. Her work in the arts, education, and activism has received national and international acclaim, from being named a 2017 Literary Arts Fellow for the State of Mississippi to serving as a U.S. arts delegate overseas. As an educator, she has authored curricula for creative writing, facilitating workshops for arts professionals, academic teachers, and audiences spanning generations.

Cherie Mays is an illustrator based out of Atlanta GA, who uses graphic design and illustration to create dynamic imagery for children's books and digital content. Early on, Cherie won awards for best illustration and use of color against nominees who were twice her age. "I was born to draw fun, vibrant characters. I absolutely love what I do." Born and raised in Kalamazoo MI, she attended college at Eastern Michigan University where she received her Bachelor's of Science degree with studies in Fine Arts and a minor in Journalism. Her journey progressed from a graphic designer in downtown Detroit to design and illustrating in Atlanta, GA. Her published books deal with categories such as bullying, epilepsy, mystery, affirmations, and more.